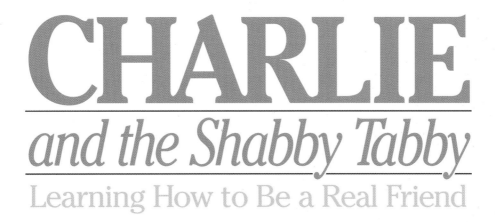

CHARLIE
and the Shabby Tabby
Learning How to Be a Real Friend

Mary Hollingsworth

as

Professor Scribbler

retells the Parable of the Good Samaritan

Illustrated By
Peeler-Rose Productions

Brownlow

Brownlow Publishing Company, Inc.

DEDICATION

To Charlie
and
children
everywhere

This Book Belong's

A SPECIAL BOOK

~~For~~
To:

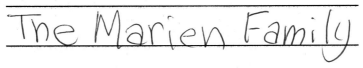

The Marien Family

From

_____

_____

_____

Date

Dear Parents and Teachers,

Jesus, the master teacher, often told simple stories from everyday life (or "parables" as we call them) to help God's children understand important spiritual truths. For example, in response to one person who was trying to find out how little he could do and still be called a "good neighbor," Jesus told the parable of the Good Samaritan.

To answer this question, Jesus said, "A man was going down the road from Jerusalem to Jericho. Some robbers attacked him. They tore off his clothes and beat him. Then they left him lying there, almost dead.

It happened that a Jewish priest was going down that road. When the priest saw the man, he walked on by on the other side of the road. Next, a Levite came there. He went over and looked at the man. Then he walked by on the other side of the road.

Then a Samaritan traveling down the road came to where the hurt man was lying. He saw the man and felt very sorry for him. The Samaritan went to him and poured olive oil and wine on his wounds and bandaged them. He put the hurt man on his donkey and took him to an inn. At the inn, the Samaritan took care of him. The next day, the Samaritan brought out two silver coins and gave them to the innkeeper. The Samaritan said, 'Take care of this man. If you spend more money on him, I will pay it back to you when I come again.'"

Then Jesus said, "Which one of these three men do you think was a neighbor to the man who was attacked by the robbers?" The teacher of the law answered, "The one who helped him." Jesus said to him, "Then go and do the same thing he did!"
(Luke 10:30-37, ICB)

The key to this parable lies in understanding the extreme hostility between Samaritans and Jews — a fact not all adults, much less children, understand. But while children cannot grasp the complexities of the conflict between Jews and Samaritans, they do understand that mice and cats are natural enemies.

Charlie and the Shabby Tabby is simply an allegory of the Good Samaritan story retold in the everyday language and experience of today's child, just as Jesus might have told it, perhaps, if he were here today. By looking at this parable through the natural antagonism of the cat and mouse relationship, which your child has seen time and again in cartoons on TV, in his early childhood literature, and even in real life, he will easily learn the true spirit of being a real friend and neighbor.

He will learn from Charlie Wandermouse and his friend Professor Scribbler that being a real friend is (1) more than just talk — it requires action and personal sacrifice, and (2) it's more than just helping our friends and people who are like us — it's helping even an enemy.

Curl up now with your child in your favorite "reading chair" and experience the exciting Adventures of Charlie Wandermouse. They are lessons for the heart.

The Publisher

Hello. I'm a writer named Professor Scribbler. And this is my best friend, Charlie Wandermouse — the world famous musician, traveler and explorer. In this story, Charlie (a mouse) puts his life . . . and mine . . . in danger to help a cat! Can you imagine such a thing? Well, just turn the page to see for yourself.

Now, Flora Flittermouse owns a boardinghouse on the banks of Flitterpond. Sometimes the pond is full, but most of the time it's almost empty.

The pond and boardinghouse are at the edge of Cheddartown and a delightful place for us writers and musicians to live.

It was a bright and sunny day.   Charlie and I
had been sitting on the porch. We were munching
on bits of cheese and wishfully looking at the pond
when we decided to go for a drive in the country.

So, we hopped into his red Race-a-Cat Turbo and headed out for a day in the country. The wind blew through our whiskers and the sun warmed our faces as we began to sing. Why, the whole countryside must have heard us. I didn't realize we knew so many songs!

As we came around Blind Mice Corner, we couldn't believe our eyes. A rusty, old, green Jaloppacat was overturned on the side of the road. The driver — a shabby, old, tabby cat — was lying in the grass. We could see that he was hurt very badly.

Charlie hit the brakes and swerved the Turbo off the road under a big mushroom to look over the problem. We could see two mean-looking alleycats sneaking away toward Catville. They must have hitched a ride with the old tabby, then robbed him, beat him up and left him in the ditch.

Now, it's not a normal thing for a mouse, even Charlie Wandermouse, to help a cat. And we could see that this cat was not from our neighborhood. So, Charlie and I were trying to decide what to do.

We couldn't just drive away and leave the poor old cat in the ditch. But if we did try to help him, he might eat us. This was not an easy decision.

Suddenly a big, flashy, blue Catalak roared around the corner. It was Dr. I. B. Furry on his way to the annual hospital party. He was talking on his mobile phone when he saw the accident and slowed down.

Charlie sighed, "Great! Dr. Furry can take better care of an injured cat than we can anyway." We were both happy things had turned out so well.

We walked back to the Turbo to drive away. But we were shocked to see Dr. Furry glance down at his watch and then drive to the other side of the road. Suddenly, he roared away, not stopping to help.

It looked as if it would be up to Charlie and me to help the hurt cat after all. I was scared and my whiskers began to twitch nervously.

Soon another car, a pink Furari, zoomed past us. Then we heard the screech of tires, and the car backed up beside the wrecked Jaloppacat.

The car was driven by Dr. Furry's nurse, Miss Kitty Softpaw. Miss Kitty is a long-haired Persian beauty who works in Intensive Cat Care at the hospital.

Once again, Charlie and I thought we had been saved from possible disaster. So, we scurried back to the Turbo to make our escape.

Then we heard Miss Kitty race the engine and squeal the tires as she sped away to the hospital party. The poor old cat was left in the ditch all alone. He had no one to help him, except Charlie and me.

Without another thought about his own safety,
Charlie jumped out of the car and scampered up to
the hurt tabby. I followed him, but I am not as brave
as Charlie is. I stayed a few scampers safely out of

the reach of the big tabby's claws. The shabby, old tabby had been knocked out. I got the first aid kit from the Turbo and Charlie bandaged the cat's head and hurt paw.

Then we called Crash-a-Cat Wrecking Service to turn the Jaloppacat right side up. About that time the cat woke up. At first, he hissed at us and licked his lips. Now this is a perfectly normal thing for a cat to do, certainly. But it was a little scarey anyway. Then, he saw that we were really trying to help him. He moaned an apology, purred a weak thank you and crawled into his shabby, old car.

While Charlie guided the huge Jaloppacat down the road, I worked the accelerator and brakes. We're quite a team, you know.

We finally arrived at Nine Lives Inn and rented a nice fur-lined room for Tom. Charlie called room service and ordered a bowl of warm milk for Tom. And we stayed with him all night in case he needed anything else.

The next day, we said good-bye to Tom Tabby who was feeling much better. Then Charlie and I paid for Tom's room. He also told the motel clerk to give Tom anything else he needed, and we would come back on Tuesday to pay for that, too. Then, with happy hearts, we drove home to Flitterpond.

Now, most folks would say that a mouse can't be a friend to a cat. It's just not natural. But who would you say was a friend to Tom? Was it Dr. I. B. Furry, Nurse Kitty Softpaw or was it Charlie Wandermouse?

What about you? What can you do this week to be a good neighbor and a friend to someone?